3.0pts

Angel's Mother's Baby

Angel's Mother's Baby

Judy Delton

Illustrated by Margot Apple

Houghton Mifflin Company
Boston

Library of Congress Cataloging-in-Publication Data

Delton, Judy.
  Angel's mother's baby / Judy Delton ; illustrated by Margot Apple.
    p. cm.
  Summary: Twelve-year-old Angel has adjusted to her mother's
remarriage and believes that she and her younger brother Rags now
live in the perfect family, until she discovers that her mother is
going to have another baby.
  ISBN 0-395-50926-2
  [1. Babies—Fiction. 2. Brothers and sisters—Fiction.
3. Remarriage—Fiction. 4. Family life—Fiction.] I. Apple,
Margot, ill. II. Title.
PZ7.D388Ao 1989   89-7544
[Fic]—dc20   CIP
               AC

Printed in the United States of America

QUM 20 19 18 17 16 15 14 13 12

For Lorna Balian:
With warm lobster, asparagus,
and Detroit memories, and the
wish you lived next door.

.

Contents

1. The "I Can't Read" Book   1
2. The Awful Kindergarten Secret   15
3. Rooftop Guests   29
4. Angel's Mother's News   44
5. Old Lady Angel   54
6. Booties for the Baby   61
7. A Family Affair   71
8. For She's a Jolly Good Fellow   84
9. Angel Takes a Spill   95
10. Baby Talk   108
11. Just a Dream   124

Angel's Mother's
Baby

1.
The "I Can't Read" Book

Angel sat in the swing on the front porch of her big green house, reading *Sue Barton, Student Nurse* and eating a Chocolate Crispie cookie. The book was boring. Angel knew she did not want to be a nurse. The cookie was good. Packed with walnuts. Her mother made lots of good things now that she worked only part-time. She worked only part-time because at last she was acting like a real mother, the mother Angel always wanted. Last August she had married a clown. His name was Rudy, and although when he was her mother's boyfriend he had worried Angel, things had finally worked out well. They were now a normal family. A shiver went down Angel's back just thinking how normal they were. One father, one mother, and two children, a boy (Rags) and a girl! Angel had read that a perfect American family was 2.5 children, but since she had a hard time picturing half a child, their two came close enough to perfection to suit her.

Her new father went off to work every morning at the TV studio where he did a children's show, and her mother smiled a lot and froze peaches and made fancy things for dinner like moo goo gai pan, instead of the TV dinners they used to have before Rudy, when she worked full-time. And Rudy oiled things that squeaked and put the chipped putty back in the windows, things her mother always said she would learn to do but never had time for.

And every morning she, Angel, got up and ate cereal and eggs and went off to school where she was in the fifth grade. Rags was in kindergarten. Poor Rags. He had just learned last year to spell his whole name, Theodore

O'Leary, when he had to start all over again, because Rudy adopted them and they had a new name. And the new name was one of the few not-quite-normal things about Rudy Pappadopolis. It ruined Angel's monogrammed clothes, but Rudy bought her new ones. It made Rags cry because it was so hard to spell. But Rudy said, what if your name was Jignioloopachinski, and that made Rags laugh, and made Pappadopolis sound short. Rudy had a way of doing that. Of making things seem funny and nothing to worry about. He did not seem to worry about anything, which was very good for Angel, because all her life she worried too much.

Rags was under the front porch. Angel could hear him. He used to play under the back porch, and had dug a city in the dirt with roads and houses and lakes and people (pretend-people) and Matchbox cars. Now he had moved to the bigger area under the front porch. He was expanding, Rudy said. Angel heard the slap, slap of dirt being excavated. And she heard her mother humming "Bridge Over Troubled Waters," one of her favorite songs. There was no doubt about it. It was very, very nice being a normal family. At last. Angel almost purred in the swing in the sun. No upsetting thing loomed on the horizon now, like her mother going on a vacation without her, or on another honeymoon, or worry about tax men from Washington coming after her mother (which had been her wild imagination all along!). No baby sitters like Alyce again, who fell off chairs and broke legs, leaving poor Angel to cope with a small child and a big house with ghosts and Rags's infernal questions about where do babies come from. And no dog laundries with large sheepdogs in their bathtub, leaving behind hair to plug up the drain. All of those old problems were in the past. Now her family was just like Edna's family. Or anyone's at school.

Down the street Angel could see Edna's

bike. She knew it was her friend Edna because she pretended her bike was a horse, and called "Giddap!" as she rode, holding on to a rope instead of the handlebars. She came closer and closer, and then dragged her feet when she got to Angel's house, and tied her horse to the fence. She climbed the porch steps and plunked herself down on the porch floor.

"I like Saturdays," she said. "All day to do stuff."

Angel liked all the days. Even school was OK this year. She put Sue Barton down without a marker. She didn't care if she lost her place.

"Nancy Drew is better," said Edna. "Or this new book called *Heather Rockwell*. It's got romance in it!"

Angel had had enough romance the last several months. Having a mother with a boyfriend, and then a wedding, was enough to last a while.

"I don't like romance," she said.

"Boy I do," said Edna. "We are getting to dating age, you know. Pretty soon."

"You're getting boy crazy like those girls at school," said Angel.

"Well, we can't stay little kids all our life," Edna said.

Edna was always onto new things before Angel, thought Angel. And she knew about things like weddings and showers and RSVPs and things Angel had never heard of. So it seemed natural she would know about romance before Angel.

"Twelve is when your body changes,"Edna said wisely. Angel knew what she meant. Her mother had given her books to read, but she didn't really understand them. Angel decided to wait till she really wanted to know about something and then ask Edna. Edna would know all about everything. And she made it all seem simple. Edna was a good person to know.

"I can't wait to get married and have babies!" Edna went on.

"Rudy says girls should be something," said Angel.

"Like a nurse?" said Edna, frowning and wrinkling her nose distastefully.

Angel glanced down at Sue Barton. "There are lots of things to be. Like an astronaut or a telephone operator. Maybe even a TV repairman, or a roofer."

Edna snorted. "I'll let my husband bring home lots of money. I'm going to marry somebody real rich."

Angel decided to change the subject. Growing up meant more change. And change was something Angel did not need more of. "Let's go to the library and take this book back," said Angel, standing up and brushing the Chocolate Crispie crumbs onto the floor.

"Can I come?" shouted a muffled voice that sounded like it was underground. Rags crawled out from under the porch and looked at Angel and Edna with his pleading look.

"Yuck," said Edna. "You're too dirty."

"Go wash, Rags. You can come if you get clean."

Rags's sandals flapped against the porch floor as he dashed into the house to get ready. He loved to go to the library. He wanted to read more than anything he could think of. He wanted to carry real books home like Angel did. Kindergarten was for babies. Reading and writing and adding up numbers was what real people did.

Rags came out with streaks on his arms and legs where the clean water had gone. His hair was wet and slicked back stiffly. "I'm ready," he said.

He put his small hand into Angel's, and the three of them started down Kilbourn Avenue to Main Street. When they got to the library Edna ran into the Skinner Room, which was where all the romance books were, Angel knew.

"You're not s'posed to take those books out till you're in sixth grade!" Angel whispered loudly.

Edna didn't seem to hear her. She just dashed in, and the swinging doors shut behind her.

Angel went down the hall to the children's room with Rags, and led him to the picture-book shelves. She picked out a book about trucks and one about snakes. They had mostly pictures and only a few words. She held one up for him to see.

Rags shook his head hard. "I want WORDS!" he said. "I don't want pictures."

"You have to have pictures, Rags," said Angel impatiently. "You can't read yet."

"Can too," said Rags with a pout.

Angel sighed. She put the snakes and trucks back on the shelf and picked up another book that was thicker. It had a picture of a boy and a dog on the cover. At the top it said, "This is an I Can Read Book."

Rags looked at the picture. He looked at how many words were in it. And he looked to see how thick it was. "What does that say?" he said pointing to the cover.

"It says, 'This is an I Can Read Book.'"

Rags took the book and held it to his chest. Angel checked it out on her card and then went to the other side of the room and looked for a book for herself.

Angel took a long time choosing a book. She kept her eye on Rags, who was sitting in one of the chairs shaped like a bear, carefully "reading" his new book. Angel found a book she liked called *Courage at Indian Deep*. It took place in Minnesota. That was not far from Wisconsin, where she lived, so she decided to check it out. There was no sign of Edna, so Angel sat down by one of the big library windows and began to read. Soon she was lost in the story and forgot where she was. All of a sudden, she heard the sound of someone crying. She looked up from her book and saw a small crowd of children around someone in the picture-book section. Probably one of the little children grabbed a book away from someone else, thought Angel. But as she opened her book again, the sobbing grew louder. The cries sounded familiar! Rags! She suddenly remembered she had taken him along to the library!

She ran over to the group of children, and sure enough, there was Rags in the middle! By now the librarian had come to see what the noise was about.

When Rags saw Angel coming, he stopped sobbing and began to wail. "You lied!" he shouted, pointing a still-dirty finger at her. "You lied to me!"

Now Rags threw himself to the floor, still wailing. Why had Angel taken him along? What a baby he still was! Kindergarten had

not helped Rags grow up. He would never grow up! Rags would be a cry baby forever! And he would always be hanging on Angel, whining and dirty.

Mrs. Mark, the librarian, was trying to reason with Rags. "Now just tell us what is the matter, Rags!" she begged. Rags only wailed more loudly. The other children watched carefully, glad it was not their small brother or sister who was making the fuss.

Angel was impatient with Rags. "Get up this minute, Rags!" she said, stamping her foot.

"You lied," he repeated.

Now all the attention turned to Angel, the accused. She bent over and picked Rags up by the back of his shirt and set him on his feet. She began to drag him toward the door, and said between her clenched teeth, "What do you mean, I lied?"

"You said I CAN READ this book, and I can't! Not one word!"

He held up the book. He was right. It did say "I Can Read."

"Rags, that means that you can read if you know how to read it!"

"It says 'I Can Read' right there," said Rags, punching the words with his fist.

Angel had to admit he was right. People that make books should be more careful what they call them. They should think before they put things on covers that are not true.

The door burst open and Edna came in. "I heard some little kid crying," she began. Then she looked at Rags. The black streaks had turned to dark rivers on his face, and he was still sniffing and sobbing.

He held up the book for Edna to see. "It says 'I Can Read.' And I can't."

"But, Rags, that means that you have to know how to —" But Rags didn't wait to hear any more. He was out the door ahead of them. He did not want to be told all kinds of excuses. It said he could read and he couldn't. That was all there was to it.

"Maybe if we read it to him," said Edna.

Angel shook her head. "He just has to grow up," she said.

But she had a feeling down deep he never would.

2.
The Awful
Kindergarten Secret

Edna left to go home, and Angel began to help her mother with dinner. A roast was already in the oven and the cozy smells of garlic and onion simmering on the meat filled the house. It smelled so much better than the TV dinners they used to have when their mother was too tired from working all day, or too rushed, to cook real dinners. Now their mashed potatoes did not have to come out of a box. They were real honest-to-goodness potatoes that had dirt on them from some Iowa farmer's field, and Rudy sat and peeled them with a sharp peeler. While Angel set the table in the dining room her mouth watered, waiting to eat. Rudy had a big white apron tied around his waist. He did as much cooking as their mother did. He loved food and he loved to eat. He swung Rags up on his shoulders and gave him a ride to the bathroom to wash up for dinner. Rags usually squealed in delight at this, but he was still upset about the I Can Read Book and pouted.

"What's the matter, old buddy?" sang Rudy, soaping up Rags's hands in the sink.

"I can't read," muttered Rags.

"That's because you are only in kindergarten," said Rudy. "No big deal. You have all your life to read. I think people read too young, do you know that? It wears out your brain cells to read at your age."

Rudy winked at Angel, who was walking down the hall to her room. Angel knew Rudy was just kidding. Reading didn't use up your brain cells.

"Save your cells, that's what I say," said Rudy.

"WANNA READ," shrieked Rags. He pouted even more.

Rudy did not take things seriously. Even serious things, thought Angel. He just laughed and hoisted Rags back up on his shoulder. He whistled as he carried him downstairs to the dining room. He bounced him onto a chair, and then went into the kitchen to tease their mother.

All through dinner, Rags pouted. He had his I Can Read Book right beside him at the table.

Rudy pretended reading was very bad for five-year-olds. "Why, I know one boy," he said, taking more mashed potatoes and gravy, "who broke out in red spots all over, from reading. He was covered with red spots."

Angel's mother frowned and said, "Really, Rudy . . ."

Angel thought Rudy was going too far.

"And another boy," Rudy went on, "read a book when he was four, and he started to itch.

Scratch scratch scratch, all day long." Here Rudy demonstrated, jiggling around in his chair and scratching imaginary itches on his knees, his elbows, and under his chin. "He scratched until he was six. Just because he wouldn't wait to read till he was in first grade."

Angel and her mother began to laugh in spite of themselves, watching Rudy scratch like a monkey. Rags didn't laugh. He didn't know whether to believe Rudy.

After dessert Angel helped with the dishes, and then everyone trooped into the living room to watch "The Cosby Show." Rags was still trying to read his book. At the commercial, Angel noticed that Rags was scratching his head. Her mother noticed too.

"Rags, stop scratching," she said.

"My hair itches," he said.

"Ha! I told you!" said Rudy. "It's that book."

"I can't read it!" cried Rags. "I can't read a word."

"Then it can't be that," said Rudy. "Are you sure you didn't read just one little word? One little word could give you one little itch."

Rags shook his head. Angel and Rags watched cartoons next. Rags seemed to forget he couldn't read. He laughed out loud at Daffy Duck. But he kept scratching.

"I think I'll wash his hair," said their mother.

"You just washed our hair yesterday," said Angel.

"I know, but Rags must have been in the sandbox," she said.

Mrs. Pappadopolis took Rags upstairs and scrubbed his head hard. Then she rubbed it dry with a towel. Rags got his pajamas on and crawled into bed. When his mother came in to kiss him good night, he was scratching his head again.

"Rags! Stop scratching!"

"I can't," he said. "My hair itches."

"It can't," said his mother. "Your hair is fresh and clean."

On Monday morning Rags was still itching and scratching.

"I am going to take Rags to see Dr. Strong," she said. "Get dressed, Rags."

Rudy left for work, calling, "Stay away from those books!" to Rags. Rags just scratched harder than ever.

"We'll drop you off at school," said her mother to Angel. "On the way to the doctor."

"Can we give Edna a ride too?" said Angel, as they got into the car. Edna was coming down the street toward Angel's house.

"Of course," said Mrs. Pappadopolis. Edna crawled into the back seat beside Angel. After they drove a few blocks, the two girls crawled out again, at their school.

Rags kept scratching.

"Don't want to go to the doctor," whined Rags. "Don't like doctors."

"Doctors make you well," said his mother. "When you're sick."

"I'm not sick," muttered Rags. "I just itch."

"Come right in," said Dr. Strong's nurse. "You're out bright and early this morning."

"He itches," said Mrs. Pappadopolis.

The nurse frowned.

"Just my hair," said Rags, climbing up on the table covered with white paper.

When the doctor came in, Rags told him the same thing. Itchy hair. The doctor laughed and took Rags's temperature. Then he examined Rags's hair and scalp. "Just what I thought," he said. "You have head lice."

Mrs. Pappadopolis screamed a small scream. "Lice!" she said.

"Everyone gets it," said the doctor. "Especially kindergarteners."

"But Rags is clean," said his mother. "I

washed his hair four times last week."

"Lice like clean hair," said Dr. Strong. "The cleaner the better. Dirty hair seems to keep them away."

The doctor was writing a prescription on a little pad of paper. "Just use this according to the directions," he said. "And keep Rags home because it is so contagious. He can go back to school when he stops itching."

Rags scratched all the way home in the car. Mrs. Pappadopolis stopped at the drugstore and got the medicine. Then she rushed home and used it as directed on Rag's head.

"Don't tell anyone about this," she whispered into his ear. "No one."

When Angel came home and asked what the doctor said, her mother said, "Oh, it's just an allergy. He gave us some medicine."

When Rudy came home, she told him the same thing. But Rudy asked questions. "Allergy to what?" he asked.

"Probably shampoo," lied Mrs. Pappadopolis. She looked worried.

That evening when Angel was doing her
homework, she began to scratch her head.
While Rudy was reading the paper he began to
scratch his head.

"I think I may have caught Rags's allergy,"
said Angel.

"Me too," said Rudy.

Mrs. Pappadopolis looked like she might
cry. "It's head lice!" she cried. "Rags brought
head lice home from kindergarten!"

Angel looked alarmed. "Bugs?" she said.
But Rudy just laughed and laughed. "Allergy," he laughed. "Head lice isn't an allergy."

"I don't want anyone to know," whispered
his wife. "I don't want anyone to know we
have lice in our family."

Angel didn't either. It would be humiliating.
"I won't tell anyone," she said.

"We can't go out," said Mrs. Pappadopolis. "It could spread. We have to stay inside until it is gone. You two can use Rags's medicine."

Angel and Rudy washed their hair with the medicine. They rubbed it in well.

"We can't go out or in," said Angel's mother. "I just hope we have enough food until it is gone."

The next morning their mother was scratching. "Now we've all got it!" she moaned.

"It could be worse," said Rudy cheerfully. "This will give us a vacation from work."

"But we can't go anywhere," their mother said.

"We'll have fun right here together!" said Rudy.

Rudy called in to work and said he had an allergy. And then there was a knock on the door. It was Edna.

"Don't let her in!" shouted Mrs. Pappadopolis. "And don't tell her what we've got!"

Angel opened the door a crack. "I can't go

to school," she said. "I'm sick." Angel closed the door.

"I'll call you after school," called Edna through the closed door.

All morning the family played games together. They had a picnic lunch together. It was fun. In the afternoon they watched TV. They had a picnic supper. And they scratched

their heads. Even when they used the medicine, they scratched their heads.

"It has to run its course," said Rudy, wisely.

The next day they didn't have as much fun.
Angel and Rags grew tired of board games.
And TV. Their mother was tired of knitting.
Even Rudy grew a little impatient when Angel
took too long putting down her word in Scrab-
ble. And at suppertime, Angel's mother said,
"There's no milk. Or bread."

"We won't starve," said Rudy cheerfully.

They wouldn't starve, thought Angel. But
she didn't want to eat funny things like tartar
sauce and noodles. Or canned beets and gra-
ham crackers.

When anyone came to the door, Angel's
mother lifted the edge of the curtain and
peered out. Then she opened the door a small
crack and said they were sick. Alyce wanted
to come in and take care of them.

"NO!" said their mother, in a too loud

voice. "Thank you anyway, though!"

That evening Edna called. She didn't seem interested in what Angel had. She just went on talking about school. "We had fractions yesterday. You are going to be way behind. And guess what? The kindergarten is closed! They had an outbreak of, get this, HEAD LICE! Can you imagine? Head lice! And last night my head started to itch. My mom says I've got it too! Can you believe it? Where would I get HEAD LICE?"

Edna slowed down, to catch her breath. Angel couldn't believe her ears.

"My mom said not to tell anyone — they will think we are dirty or something. But if the whole kindergarten has it —"

"Edna, you got it from us! From Rags! My mom didn't want us to tell either."

Edna didn't even seem surprised. "If you've got it too, I can come over," she said. "I hate being shut up in the house all day. I mean, I'm not sick, you know."

"Come over!" said Angel, hanging up the phone.

"Edna's coming over," said Angel to her mother.

Her mother began to speak, but Angel said, "She's got it too! Edna's got head lice! The whole kindergarten has it!"

Mrs. Pappadopolis began to laugh. Rudy began to laugh. Angel started to laugh too. The only one not laughing was Rags.

"You said not to tell," he said. "And the whole kindergarten doesn't have head lice. I don't!" Rags pointed to his head. "I don't itch anymore!" he said. "My allergy is all gone!"

Rudy grabbed Rags by his shoulders and hoisted him up on his own shoulders. "Well, don't let me see you reading again, young man. I don't want this to come back again!"

3.
Rooftop
Guests

Finally all of Angel's family, and Edna too, stopped itching. In a little while they even forgot how embarrassing it was to have lice. "Misery loves company," said Alyce when she heard about it. Alyce was her mother's best friend. She always had a saying for anything that happened. "Trouble shared is trouble halved," she often said.

One day after school Edna came home with Angel. The girls did their homework to the sound of Rudy's pounding. Rudy was putting a new drainpipe up the side of the house. His hammer hitting the tin pipe made a deafening noise. Edna put her hands over her ears.

"Why is Rudy always pounding some-thing?" she asked.

"He says everything around here needs work," said Angel. "He put putty around the glass in my window, and he put a new faucet in the bathroom. Now it doesn't drip," she said.

Edna glanced at a toolbox on the floor. And there was a metal tape measure and a level and a piece of pipe beside it. "Can he do every-thing?" said Edna.

"Almost." said Angel. "He said we need a new roof though, and he can't put that on."

"We have to have workmen come in to fix things," said Edna. "My dad can't pound a nail in straight, my mom says."

Angel felt lucky, in more ways than one, to have Rudy in the family. He was a good father, and he made her mother very happy. And he loved to work around the house. "Rudy says, 'If you want something done right, you have to do it yourself,'" said Angel.

"This is a big house," said Edna. "Bigger than ours. You could have piles of brothers and sisters, living here."

Angel stared at her. What did she mean? She did not need any more brothers and sisters. She had the perfect family. Two children was perfect. "I have a brother," said Angel.

"Just one," said Edna, waving her arm, as if only one sibling was not enough. "You could have tons of kids in this house. Now that you've got a father." She paused. "You couldn't have more kids without a father," she added.

Angel was getting cross with Edna. The idea! Thinking Angel needed more brothers and sisters. What about her — Edna. She had *no* brothers and sisters. She was the one who should be thinking of a bigger family.

"Your house is plenty big," said Angel. "How come you don't have more kids? You've got a father."

Edna looked like she was dying to tell Angel. "My mom and dad can't have any more kids," she said. "They went to the doctor and everything. The doctor said they were lucky to have ME!"

Angel was impressed. "Why?" she asked. "Why can't they have more?"

"Tubes or something," said Edna. "My mom said they tried and tried and no luck. They'd have to adopt kids if they wanted more.

"Let's play Scrabble, I'm tired of doing homework," said Edna, changing the subject.

Angel didn't feel like playing Scrabble. Edna's words had disturbed her. She couldn't bear to think of a houseful of children. Would this happen? Did fathers want a lot of children? Did they come automatically when there was a father in the house? The house was not as big as Edna made it sound. And Angel hated change of any kind. Things were just fine the way they were.

Angel's mother and Rudy and Rags burst in the door. They looked smiling and happy. They had burgers for everyone for supper. "For Edna too," her mother said. Edna called her mother. She said she could stay.

"I hope it pours," said Rudy. "So we can try out our new drainpipe."

"If it pours, the roof will leak," said Angel's mother. Rudy snapped his fingers. "I have to get that guy from Tom's Roofing out to look at the roof," he said, walking into the kitchen for the phone book.

"Why don't you stay overnight?" said Angel's mother to Edna after supper.

"OK," said Edna, calling her mother again.

Angel frowned. She liked Edna. But she didn't like her mom inviting her friends to stay over without asking her. After all, she was Angel's friend, not her mom's.

"She says fine," said Edna with a smile.

Edna wanted to talk all night. Angel didn't. Somehow she still felt cross about the brothers-and-sisters talk. There was a nagging little worry in the back of her head now that wouldn't let her alone. These little worries often got inside her head and kept her from happy, carefree feelings. It was like the time she had a tooth that ached, thought Angel. It went away when her mom gave her a baby aspirin, but after a few hours there it was again, popping up and ruining a perfectly good afternoon at the beach.

In the morning Angel's mother stuck her head in the door of Angel's room and whispered, "Rudy and I are going to the sale at Hardware Herb. You just sleep late," she said, closing the door.

Angel turned over and went back to sleep. It was Saturday and there was no school. Angel began to dream that her house was packed with people. More and more people moved in. Besides the people, there were animals living there! Dogs and geese and pet mice and even a goat with whiskers. As the house filled, the walls bulged out. The house got fatter and fatter until, POP! It exploded! The roof fell in, kerplunk! Her mother's leaky roof! The loud noise woke Angel up. She sat up in bed and told herself it was only a dream.

If it was a dream, what was the noise she heard now? A noise on the roof! Right over her head. Scrape, drag, scrape. Something sounded only inches away! This was no dream. Angel shook Edna.

"It's Saturday," moaned Edna. "We can sleep late."

"Edna! Listen! What is that noise?"

Edna sat up in bed. Scrape drag scrape. There it was again.

Edna looked up at the ceiling. "Footsteps!" she said. "On the roof!" Edna was always right. If she said footsteps, those were footsteps. But footsteps were on sidewalks. On the ground. Or in a house. Not on *top* of a house. "Who would walk on top of a *roof*?" said Edna.

The girls ran to the window. They could not see anyone. "They are on top of us!" cried Angel. "We won't be able to see them!"

"Nobody walks on top of a roof," said Edna sensibly. Then they both thought of the same thing. Rags. Rags might walk on a roof. They leaped out of bed and ran to his room. "He's in bed!" cried Angel. Sure enough, Rags was sleeping peacefully. He was definitely not on the roof.

When the girls got back to Angel's room, they heard voices. Voices as close as close could be. "Hey!" shouted one voice. "Over here, bring it over here!"

Bring what over here? thought Angel. Drag drag drag. Now it sounded like someone was sawing wood! In Angel's closet!

"Don't open that door!" Angel shouted, to Edna. "It must be a burglar! Coming in through my closet to rob us!"

"Two burglars!" corrected Edna. "There are two burglars making a hole in the roof!"

Angel wanted to hide under the covers. But that was silly. They would not be safe there. And Rags, poor little Rags. He had to be protected. "We have to do something," said Angel.

Edna nodded. "I'm thinking," she said.

It was suddenly quiet in the room. The sawing had stopped! Then a voice sounded again, a few feet away from the girls, it seemed. "Naw," it said. "Let's try over here." The footsteps walked over their heads. Drag, went something behind them.

"They are going to try to make a hole someplace else," said Edna.

"Maybe they couldn't get through my closet," said Angel.

Now there was a new sound. The squeaky sound of a hammer pulling up long nails!

"They are taking the shingles off," whispered Edna. "So they can get in."

Angel wanted to scream, but she did not want the men to hear them. "Maybe they think no one is home," said Angel. "They think they are robbing an empty home. They might murder us!"

"I think we should wake up Rags and get out," said Edna.

Angel shook her head vigorously. "No," she said. "They'll see us running away and they'll shoot us from the roof."

"Then what will we do?" moaned Edna.

The girls thought. Then Angel snapped her fingers. "Call 911," she said. "In any emergency we are s'posed to call 911." Angel's mother had told them that often. Dialing 911 would bring help.

Edna flew to the phone in the hall. She dialed 911. It rang and rang. "Operator," said a voice. "What is your emergency?"

"Burglars!" shouted Edna. "Send the police right away. Some burglars are making a hole in the roof and coming in," she said.

"In the roof?" said the voice.

"Send the police," repeated Edna. What

difference did it make where they were coming in? A window or door or the roof?

"Address," said the operator. She seemed sleepy.

Edna gave her the address. Then she added, "It's on Kilbourn Avenue and Brownell Street. On the corner. It's a big green house. With a fence and petunias."

"There are no petunias yet," whispered Angel. "Petunias don't grow till summer."

Edna hung up. "Should we wake up Rags?" she said.

Angel thought. Rags was a lot of work when he was awake. He would want to eat, even in an emergency. "We'd better let him sleep. If the police catch the burglars and take them to jail, there isn't any need for Rags to get up."

The girls got dressed while the scraping sounds and shouting went on overhead. "Wouldn't you think they'd be quiet if they are robbing a house?" said Edna, with her foamy toothbrush in her mouth.

"How can you brush your teeth when the police are coming?" demanded Angel.

"Tartar buildup," said Edna. "I have to floss too. Every day. No matter what."

When the girls were dressed they crept downstairs to the front door. Just as they got there, they heard loud sirens coming down Kilbourn Avenue.

"Here they come!" shouted Edna. "I hope they get those guys before they get away. They should sneak up on them. They shouldn't blow their sirens!"

A screaming police car pulled up in front of the house, with red lights flashing. Angel had a fleeting thought that it was too bad Rags was missing this excitement. He loved police cars. Then another flashing car came. And another! And last of all, a large red fire engine with hoses and men in big hats and a dog on the running board pulled up.

The girls ran out into the front yard. "Up

there!" they yelled, pointing to the rooftop. "Up there!"

Angel looked up at the roof to see if the burglars had gotten away. No, there they were! Not even trying to escape. They were just standing on the roof watching the excitement. One had an ax in his hand. The other had a long metal measuring tape. On their heads were white hard hats.

"Where is the criminal?" shouted the police, pouring out of their squad cars, guns drawn.

"There they are!" the girls shouted again and pointed.

The men on the roof looked behind them. The police shouted, "What are you doing up there?"

"Who, us?" said one of the men, pointing to himself. "We're here to check the roof for new shingles," he said. "We're from Tom's Roofing. I'm Tom."

The firemen were unrolling the long hose, and coming toward the house with axes. Angel's nice green house. Her green house that was not on fire. And right behind the fire truck, another car drove up. It was Alyce. And behind her were Rudy and Angel's mother. The whole neighborhood had gathered in the street. Angel wondered where they had all come from so fast.

Angel looked at Edna. "I think we made a mistake," she said.

4.
Angel's Mother's News

"Is the house on fire?" shouted Angel's mother, dashing across the street to the house.

"No," said Angel. She knew the next question her mother asked would be, "Then why is a fire truck here?" She did. Angel did not know herself why the fire truck was there! The roof men stood at the edge of the roof, watching all the activity.

"Fake burglars," muttered Edna. "They aren't even real."

Angel was angry at the impostors too, but she knew it wasn't their fault. They were not pretending to be burglars after all. They were being regular roof men.

Rudy came running after Angel's mother. "It's all my fault," he said, realizing what had happened. "I never thought the roof men would come before we got back!"

Rudy ran to explain to the firemen that it was a false alarm and stopped them just before they took an ax to the front door. They seemed put out that there was no fire. But they turned around and dragged their hose back to the truck. "Here, Spot," one of them said, and whistled. "The people made a mistake. C'mon, boy!"

Angel felt angry. "The people" did not make a mistake. Who asked for the fire department anyway? Operator 911, that's who. Why did she call a fire engine when Edna distinctly said "Burglars"?

Angel and Edna explained the noises and the voices and the sawing and squeaking, while a crowd of people listened. As they talked, some of the onlookers laughed and walked away. It was embarrassing. The crowd was all prepared for a fire, and Angel let them down.

"You did just the right thing," said Rudy. "You and Edna acted in a very responsible way."

Angel wiped a tear away from her eye. Rudy always stood by Angel's mistakes. Even Angel knew the roofers were not going to rob them.

"We left the house in good hands," said Rudy. Angel's mother looked doubtful.

"Rags!" she said. "Where is Rags?" She dashed into the not-burning house, calling his name. There was no answer.

"He's still sleeping," called Angel. The girls ran upstairs, and sure enough, through all the noise and draggings and scrapings and sirens and crowds, Rags slept on.

"I dreamed a fire engine came," he said, rubbing his eyes.

"It did!" said Angel. "And police cars."

When Angel and Edna and Rags came

downstairs with Mrs. Pappadopolis, Rudy was serving coffee and doughnuts to the roofers and policemen and some of the onlookers who had not left. It looked like a party! Rags and Edna joined right in. Angel did not feel like a party. It was her mistake. She did not think it was a time to celebrate.

Rags was sitting on a policeman's lap now, playing with his whistle. Alyce came over to Angel and handed her a doughnut. Angel shook her head.

"Let's see a big smile," said Alyce, putting a hand on Angel's shoulder. Angel shook her head. She did not feel like smiling.

"No use crying over spilled milk!" sang Alyce. "No damage done!" she added cheerfully. "No smoke! No fire!"

Finally the people drifted out the door, shaking Rudy's hand and chuckling. Even Edna said good-bye and drifted out the door. Probably in a hurry to get home and tell her mother the whole story, thought Angel.

"Now," said Angel's mother. "I have a doctor's appointment this afternoon. It's time I get ready for it."

Angel forgot the roof crisis faster than she thought she could. Doctor? Why was her mother going to see the doctor? Angel had never known her mother to go to the doctor, unless she took Angel for a shot, or Rags for a sore throat. Angel stole a glance at her mother to see if she was pale. Or losing weight. Or if she had a red rash on her arms. No, her mother's face was pink and flushed and very healthy-looking. And the belt on her slacks was in the last notch. If anything, it looked like her mother had gained some weight. The slacks fit tightly, Angel noticed, and pulled snugly around her waist.

"I don't want to go to the doctor," Rags was wailing.

"You aren't going to the doctor," called his mother from upstairs. "You and Angel can stay home. We won't be gone long."

Now Angel's mother put her head over the banister. "No roof men will be coming," she said with a small smile on her lips.

Angel wanted to shout out, "Why are you going to the doctor?" but she did not want to appear worried again. Twice in one day. If her mother was sick, it would worry her too. While she was wondering how to find out, Rags solved the problem.

"Why are you going to the doctor?" he asked suspiciously. He probably thinks she is going to get pills for him, thought Angel. Baby Rags, always thinking he's the most important person in the family. In the world, for that matter.

"Just a checkup," called their mother.

Rags seemed satisfied at his mother's words and went off singing, "Checkup, checkup, stickup, pickup," in what his mother often called his "creative mood."

But Angel was not easily put off. Her mother often said, "Don't fix something that works." When Rudy wanted to take the car in for a checkup, she remembered her mother saying, "It runs fine. If you take it in they'll find something the matter."

Wasn't a car like a person? Angel never remembered her mother going to the doctor before, for a checkup.

Mrs. Pappadopolis came running down the stairs, pink and rosy from the shower, with her hair in a ponytail like a young girl. She gave Angel a hug and a kiss and said, "We'll be right back."

Rudy waved and said, "Don't take any wooden nickels," and they were off.

Angel felt restless while her parents were gone. She watched TV a while and read a story to Rags. Then she sighed and fell asleep on the living room couch. She dreamed that her mother came home from the doctor on crutches, and with a big white bandage around her head. As she hobbled into the house, she called cheerfully to Angel and Rags. "I'm fine!

Just had a checkup. Nothing the matter!"

But as Angel could see, in the dream, there was something the matter! Poor mother, thought Angel. Trying to be so brave. Keeping up a front for the children. As the dream went on, things got worse. It appeared that her mother could not see. Rudy brought a Seeing Eye dog in from the car.

"It's all right!" said their mother. "I'm fine. Just fine. You will be my eyes for me, Angel."

Rags was using his mother's crutches now, swinging between them like an ape, from tree to tree. Rags never took things seriously. It was up to Angel to worry for all of them. Even Rudy seemed jovial, as he threw a Frisbee for the Seeing Eye dog to catch. The dog slid into a lamp, and it came tumbling down with a crash. The crash woke Angel up.

But the crash came from the back door. Angel's mother was home. She called to her brightly, just like in the dream. "Hi. We're home!"

Angel was afraid to look. Were those her mother's crutches making all the noise? Was she blind and bandaged?

When her mother came into the living room, Angel felt a surge of relief. She looked the same as ever. "What was that noise?" said Angel. "It sounded like crutches falling, or a lamp falling over."

Mrs. Pappadopolis looked at Angel, frowning. "What ever made you think of that?" she said. "Rudy just dropped a package on the floor when he opened the door."

Rudy came in and grabbed Rags and tossed him in the air over his head. "We have some good news!" he said.

Good news? thought Angel. What kind of good news could they get at the doctor's?

Angel's mother was blushing. Her face looked pink and happy. "Sit down in the living room," she said.

Her mother led the three of them to chairs around the artificial fireplace. Then Rudy repeated his words. "I have some good news," he said again. "We are going to have a new baby in the family."

5.
Old Lady Angel

"Where is it?" demanded Rags, looking around the room and out the door toward the car.

"Not yet." His mother laughed. "Babies don't come that fast. Not for months."

Months meant forever to Rags. He lost interest immediately and went to play with his miniature cars.

Angel wondered if she was still asleep and this was part of the crutch and bandage dream. But she felt as awake as could be. It was real. Rudy really had said those words. Baby. They *had* a baby. Rags was a baby.

Her mother was looking at her. Expecting

her to be as happy and excited as she was.

Like when she told her that she was going to marry Rudy. It felt the same. Her mother wanted her to be happy. And she wasn't. She was angry. How could her mother do this to her? Just when things were settled, why would she do something so unsettling? She had a perfect husband and two fine children. How could she want more? Three children was not the perfect family. It was one half too many.

"Angel?" said her mother, with a worried look on her face.

But Angel just stared at her mother's jingly silver heart bracelet. The sun was shining on it, and it flashed in Angel's eyes like those things they swing on a chain to put you in a trance. It jingled and tinkled, and Angel thought to herself that she would never forget this minute. The minute that changed her life. That made her age before her time. Barely twelve, but an old lady. Old lady Angel. She was sure gray hair was sprouting at her roots.

Jingle jingle. Tinkle tinkle. All she could think
of was the bracelet in the sun.

Her mother came over and shook her by the
shoulder. "Are you all right?" she said.

No, Angel wanted to scream. No, I'm not
all right.

Rudy began to say something, but Angel's
mother motioned him out. Then she sat down
by Angel and stroked her hair. Jingle, jingle
went the silver bracelet again.

"Aren't we enough?" demanded Angel. "Rags and me?"

"Of course you're enough," said her mother. "But you aren't babies anymore."

Angel thought about that. Did that mean that when a baby grew up you had to have another one right away to replace it? At that rate a person would be having babies forever!

"Rudy has never had a tiny baby of his own. And a new baby in the house will make it so cheerful, Angel. Just think of a smiling baby, learning to talk and walk and learn things. It will keep us all young!"

Angel didn't want to be kept young. And Rags was young enough already. Was her mother forgetting that with the smiles and walking and talking came dirty diapers and crying all night? It wasn't that long ago that Rags had gotten rid of his soggy pacifier and wet diapers and those awful nursing bottles around the house with warm milk in them. Rags was in school now! Her mother had gotten rid of the crib and the bottles and buggy. Angel and Rags were way too old to have a baby brother or sister. Their mother should be selling Tupperware now, or working full-time, or trying those new gourmet recipes for their dinner from Alyce's magazines. Instead of that, they would be having TV dinners again while their mother, tired and crabby from nights with the baby, tried to get some rest. Angel sighed. It was too much for her small shoulders. She was too old for a sister and too young for a mother. And she felt like she would be playing mother a lot of the time to this baby.

"It will be fun, Angel," her mother was saying.

Her mother's reasons for this baby were flimsy.

"I know it is a shock to you. You will need time to get used to the idea."

A lot of time, thought Angel. Forever. By that time she'd be gone. She might be gone tomorrow. She'd run away. Live with Edna. No, in a different town where she would not have to see her mother and Rudy and Rags and this new baby that was replacing her. Angel would get out the atlas and find a place to go.

"I know you don't like change, Angel," her mother said now. "But things can't always stay the same. Families change. The world changes."

"Our family just did change," shouted Angel. "It doesn't have to change every year!"

Angel's mother could see that being reasonable was not going to work. "I'll let you get used to the idea by yourself," she said. She got up and left the room.

Angel ran to her room and shut her door. Her wonderful little room that she first lent to Rudy, now she would probably be sharing with a baby. A screaming baby. Angel buried her head in the pillow on her bed. Only this morning, all she had to worry about was her mother on crutches, or wrapped in bandages. If only her mother had come home on crutches! If only she was wrapped in bandages! People learned to walk again without crutches. And they got well and took off bandages and threw them away.

But a baby would be with them forever.

6.
Booties for the Baby

The next few weeks, while baby plans went on around her, Angel studied maps trying to find a place to run away to. It looked hopeless. What would she do for money? Who would take her in? She would have to live on the street, or under a bridge, which felt even worse than living with a new baby. Rags had forgotten all about the baby, and was busy at school learning to write his new name, which was not easy. Rudy kept trying to cheer Angel up by telling her jokes and tweaking her nose and taking her to Smiley's for hamburgers and French fries. And her mother was so happy talking baby talk that she may as well not have two other children at all, thought Angel.

I could go to my grandma's, thought Angel. Or to Alyce's or Margaret Toomer's. They would surely take her in. The only thing is, they would say, "I have to take you home, Angel. Your family misses you and loves you," after the first day. They would not understand that they did not miss her or love her or need her.

While Angel tried to work out a plan in her head, the winter days went by. Paint was picked out for the "nursery," and Rudy was busy in the basement, building a cradle. He measured and drilled and sawed, and a pile of wood shavings piled up on the floor. Angel's mother outgrew her jeans and began to wear loose dresses and put her hand on her stomach. When she walked, she leaned backward.

Rags's old highchair came up from the basement to be scrubbed, and stood in the kitchen. When Angel opened the linen closet to get a towel, one shelf was filled with diapers. This baby was taking over the entire house, and it wasn't even born yet, Angel noticed. She waited to be told she would have to give up her room or have Rags move in with her.

But it turned out that the baby was to have the little guest room, the room her mother used for sewing. And Rudy used for paying the bills.

"It's just right!" said their mother. "Cozy and small." Her parents moved in a little chest of drawers filled with tiny undershirts and put a rug on the floor with Little Bo Peep and her sheep and a lamp in the shape of Humpty Dumpty. Rudy refinished a table to bathe the baby on.

Rags's old rocking horse got a new coat of varnish and stood in one corner. Angel could not believe how fast the house went from her old green house to a house where a baby lived. Every time she came home from school there was another new baby item.

Angel had not told Edna about the baby. She didn't want to explain. Or listen to Edna tell about her relatives that had babies. And then one day on the way home from school, Edna said, "How come you don't tell me about your mom's new baby?"

"I don't feel like it," said Angel. "Anyway, you already know." Edna always seemed to know everything about everything without being told. It made Angel feel like a baby herself to listen to Edna. "Who told you?" demanded Angel.

Edna sighed loudly. "I can see it," she said. "I can see that your mother is pregnant."

Pregnant was a word Angel was uncomfortable with. "Have a baby" was one thing. But *pregnant* fell into the gray area of words her mother might frown on if she or Rags said them. *Pregnant* was a grown-up word. Besides, how could Edna tell by looking at her mother? She looked the same as she always did.

"She's fat," said Edna, seeing the puzzled look on Angel's face.

Angel knew her mother's belt was tight, and that she wore looser clothes now, but she had not noticed that her mother was "fat." Suddenly she felt defensive for her poor mother. No one should call her mother fat and get away with it.

"Anyway, everybody knows," went on Edna. "And you've got all this baby stuff in your house. Is it s'posed to be a secret?"

Yes, thought Angel. No one should know. She didn't even want to know herself. Angel felt that if no one knew, it wasn't real. Ignore it, as Alyce so often said, and it will go away. But babies didn't go away.

"I think it's dumb not to talk about it," said Edna. "If we had a baby in our family I'd talk about it a lot."

"You would?" said Angel. "You'd like to have a baby?"

Edna nodded. "I hate being an only kid."

Another of Alyce's sayings came to Angel's mind. "You could have knocked me over with a feather," she often said when she was surprised about something. Well, Angel was surprised. Edna, jealous of *her*! Not wanting all the attention of an only child.

"On Christmas," Edna went on, "everyone has lots of kids around, screaming and yelling, and there's this paper and stuff all over. And they play games. I never have anyone to play my Christmas games with. And we just open our presents and put the paper in the wastebasket really neat. It's boring." Edna gave her eyes a wipe with the back of her hand.

Could Edna be *crying*? Were those tears she was wiping? How could anyone actually want babies, even cry for them?

"You'd have to baby-sit and heat up bottles and have smelly diapers around, and your mom would be real tired," said Angel.

"I'd help!" said Edna, who was crying in

earnest now. "Everybody gets to have babies but us. I'd love to take care of a baby and buy it little rattles and teach it to talk and walk and stuff," said Edna, sniffling.

Angel put her arm around Edna. "Well, I am a lot of help," said Angel. "And they will need a lot of help because Rags is still pretty little. He's a baby himself."

"And my mom keeps wanting me to do stuff with her and wanting us to get mother-daughter dresses and she still wants to comb my hair and pick out my clothes, oh it's awful!" Edna continued, weeping. "She needs a baby. She won't let me do anything by myself."

It wasn't often that Edna let this side of her life show, thought Angel. She thought Edna had lots of freedom, and was so grown-up.

"You can help me take care of the new baby," said Angel. "We can push the stroller. You can even pretend it's your baby!"

Edna brightened for a moment. "That will be fun," she said. "But it's not the same as having your own."

Edna was right. A borrowed baby was not your little sister. She didn't have the same dimples and curls and no one said, "The baby looks just like Edna at that age." At night there was no cradle to rock while you watched TV or gurgling baby smiling up from his crib in the morning. Angel remembered this when Rags was small. How had she forgotten those good things? Rags toddling around the house, weaving back and forth learning to walk. Rags reaching out his little arms to Angel when Alyce tried to hold him. Rags running to Angel when the dog next door got out of the fence.

The girls had come to Angel's house. "I have to go in," said Angel. "I'll see you later."

Edna went on to her own home, with tear stains on her face. Angel ran up the back steps and into the house. She slammed the door and called out for her mom.

"Up here, Angel!" her mother's familiar voice called.

Angel flew up the stairs and into her mother's outstretched arms. "What is it?" asked her mother. "What is it, Angel?"

"I want some yarn," said Angel, still hugging her mother. "I want to knit something for the baby. Do you think I could knit booties?"

Angel's mother looked surprised. And happy.

"I learned to knit in Scouts," added Angel.

"I think I have directions for a very easy pair of booties," said her mother. "And there is some pink yarn in my knitting bag. I'll help you get started."

"I'd like to start tonight," said Angel. Spring would be here before they knew it. And there was a lot to do before then. A lot to do to get ready for a new baby.

7.
A Family Affair

The days were going fast. Angel's mother was getting bigger and bigger. She let Rags pat her stomach and talk to the baby.

"How did you get in there, baby?" he asked it over and over again. Her mother was going to have to answer Rags soon, thought Angel. She couldn't just hand him a book, as she had done with Angel. Rags could read a few words since their library visit, but he could never read a book about where babies came from.

Angel kept knitting the booties. She got lots of knots in them but her mother showed her how to hide them.

"I wish I'd made something that was just

plain and straight," she said to Edna one day. "These are hard to knit."

"Nothing is straight for a baby," said Edna. "It can't wear a tie or a scarf or a belt."

The girls laughed at the thought of a tiny baby with a big belt.

As they were talking, Alyce drove up to the door. She had something very bulky in the car. Part of whatever it was was sticking out of the car windows.

"Just look what I got at the rummage sale at church," called Alyce. She began to tug at the mysterious thing in the car.

"And it was a wonderful buy. I just couldn't pass it up!" she went on. She got part of the thing out of the door, and then another part got stuck. Suddenly the thing started to play "Twinkle Twinkle, Little Star," and Alyce began to sing as she unloaded the object.

"Up above the world so high. Like a diamond in the sky. . ." sang Alyce, a little off key Angel thought.

Mrs. Pappadopolis appeared on the back porch.

"I have a surprise for you!" sang Alyce.

Angel's mother laughed. "If you have many more surprises, we'll have to add on to the house," she said.

Last week Alyce had brought over a large rubber Bathinette that folded up, "out of the way for storage." And the week before that she brought an old baby wardrobe of her nephew's. "Rudy can fix it up," she'd said. "It just needs some new hinges and it will be as good as new."

The girls ran to help Alyce unload this new monster gift. They tugged and pulled and at last it popped out of the car on top of them.

"What in the world is it?" asked Angel.

"I know!" said Edna. Of course Edna knew! She knew all about weddings and taxes and boys. It made sense that she would know all about babies.

"It's a windup swing!" she said. Alyce nodded. She pulled some long poles apart, and it stood up. Then she turned a key, and the swing hanging from the poles began to go back and forth, back and forth, while the music played.

"Allan will love this!" said Alyce. "He will have many happy hours swinging while you are busy making his meals."

"Who's Allan?" whispered Edna.

"She thinks the baby is going to be a boy," said Angel. "And she likes the name Allan."

It took Edna and Angel and Alyce and Rags to carry in the big swing. "It seems awfully big for one little baby," said Edna.

"He'll love it," said Alyce, waving away Edna's complaint with her hand.

Alyce dropped into a chair and sighed. "I see there are classes beginning at the city hall, on 'Getting Ready for That Baby.'"

"We are all signed up," said Angel's mother. "It starts tomorrow night."

"We're all going," explained Angel. "It's for the whole family."

"And Wednesday is our natural childbirth class," said Mrs. Pappadopolis.

Angel wondered what *un*natural childbirth would be like. She didn't want to ask. Edna and her mother would think she was a baby.

"Well, I think the important thing," said Alyce, "is a name for the baby. Personally I vote for Allan if it is a boy."

"Rudy likes David," said their mother. "I like Nigel, and Angel likes Kenneth."

"I like Burt," said Rags. "Name him Burt, Mom."

Burt was the name of someone in a book Rags liked. He wanted to name everything Burt.

I hope it's a girl, thought Angel. She wasn't sure she could go through another Rags-like babyhood again. Rags was such a — baby. Even when he got to be four.

"Well, I have to hit the road," said Alyce, getting up. "I have things to do. By the way, I'd like you to stop over at my house on Friday night if you can. All of you. I'd like you to see my new couch."

"You didn't mention your new couch," said Angel's mother in surprise. "Did you just get it?"

Alyce looked vague. "Oh, the other day," she said. "But be there right at seven."

"Why do we have to be there right at seven, just to see a couch?" asked Angel.

Her mother smiled. "I don't think there is any couch," she said. "I think Alyce has something up her sleeve."

Alyce almost always had something up her sleeve, thought Angel. And it was always something they were not expecting!

The next day Angel felt nervous about going to the baby classes. Maybe she should tell her mom and Rudy she had too much homework. Or that she felt a cold coming on. But at supper Rudy said, "Tonight we will all learn how to change a diaper, I'll bet!" He looked so happy about it that Angel did not have the heart to say she would rather do homework than change a diaper.

"Me too?" said Rags. "Can I change a diaper too?"

Rags change a diaper? thought Angel. He was barely out of diapers himself.

But Rudy said cheerfully, "You bet, ole buddy! This is a family project. We all get to help."

When the Pappadopolises got to the classroom, many families were already there. Angel saw a boy from her class with his parents.

"Hey, I didn't know your mom was pregnant!" he said.

There it was again. That grown-up word. "I didn't know — about your mom either," Angel said.

It was good to know Angel's family was not the only one producing babies.

All the mothers there looked as fat as her own mother, Angel noticed. Some of them looked tired. And some of the fathers were yawning. Angel wondered if they were tired from working all day, or if they were bored, coming to baby classes.

The teacher came out and welcomed the large group of expectant families. She had a large rubber doll that she put on a Bathinette like the one Alyce had given them.

"Having a baby," she said, "is definitely a family affair." Well, Angel knew that already. Why else would they all be there?

"A baby changes a family's entire lifestyle," she went on. Angel wondered what a lifestyle was and if she had one.

After she talked a long time about how to adjust to the change, the teacher went on to say how the whole family must care for the baby, not just the mother.

She showed them how to hold a baby and support its head. She showed them how to pick one up. "It won't fall apart," she said with a laugh. The crowd tittered politely.

She gave feeding hints and bathing hints and talked about symptoms of illness. She told them what to buy and what to borrow and how to know when your baby was getting teeth.

She heated a baby bottle of milk and shook it on the back of Rags's hand to show how warm to have it.

One little girl called out, "My mom is going to nurse. We don't use bottles."

"My aunt's a nurse," answered Rags proudly.

"No, no, nursing a baby is breast-feeding," said the teacher clearly.

Angel realized that this was a teacher who would also use the word *pregnant*. She would not use made-up words for parts of the body. She meant business.

"If you breast-feed your baby, then of course only the mother can feed it," said the teacher, smiling.

The class tittered again.

"Why?" called out Rags. Angel's face turned red. Why didn't her mother *tell* things to Rags?

"Because dads and kids don't have breasts," shouted out the same little girl who had brought this awful subject up. She looked about Rags's age, thought Angel. Her mother surely did a better job of telling her things than Angel's mother.

Rags looked stunned. The teacher was talking about the best kind of nipples to buy. Angel could see the questions forming in Rags's mind.

"Now," said the teacher, "we will take turns diapering this baby."

The little girl who knew so much ran to the front of the room. "Can I be first?" she said.

The teacher nodded. The little girl (whose name was Emma, Angel discovered) lifted the doll's legs skillfully and swept a diaper under it. Snap, snap went her busy hands.

"Perfect!" said the teacher. "I couldn't have done better myself.

Angel had never put a diaper on a baby. She wanted to run out the door.

"A little tighter," the teacher was telling one father. "We don't want it to fall off when you pick her up!"

Snicker snicker.

I'm glad Edna isn't here, thought Angel when it was her turn. Just as Angel was trying to get the ends together, who leaned in the doorway and waved, but Edna! She came up to the front of the room to watch.

"What are you doing here?" whispered Angel.

"My dad has a meeting down the hall," she said.

Edna sat down in the front row.

"That is very nice," said the teacher when Angel had finished. "There is only one thing the matter. You have the diaper upside down.

The plastic must go on the *outside* of the baby."

Now the room did not titter. It roared! Angel turned red as could be.

"That's an easy mistake," said Edna from the audience. "I did that when I first started to baby-sit."

Angel crept to her seat. Rudy put his arm around her. When it was his turn, he had the diaper too tight.

"See," said Edna. "No one can do it right the first time."

Rags did not want to try to put the diaper on the doll. He was still pouting about what the little girl had said.

"Why don't I?" he was muttering. "Why don't I have breasts, anyway?"

"We'll talk about it at home," said his mother softly.

Home, thought Angel. She couldn't wait to be there!

8.
For She's a Jolly Good Fellow

Angel wasn't sure she wanted to go to any more baby things. But after she practiced diapering a baby (with an old doll from the attic), she was surprised how easy it was.

"It will be so much fun with a real baby!" her mother said.

"A real baby will be soft and cuddly and smile," said Edna, who was watching. "It won't be all stiff and hard like this old doll."

On Friday afternoon, Angel said, "Remember we have to go see Alyce's new couch at seven o'clock."

Mrs. Pappadopolis frowned. "We'd better

have a bath and put on some good clothes,"
she said.

"To see a couch?" shouted Rags. "A couch
won't know if we are dressed up or not."

Rags didn't know anything about going visiting, thought Angel. Their mother had a lot to
teach him. It would take years, she thought
with a deep sigh.

"I'm suspicious of Alyce," said their
mother. "She was so insistent that we come
right at seven. We had better be prepared."

"What do you think she has up her sleeve?"
asked Angel.

"Up her sleeve, up her sleeve!" roared
Rags, putting his nose in the sleeve of his shirt.

"I think it's some sort of surprise," said
their mother. "But I don't know what."

Angel took a bath in her new bubble bath.
She put on a frilly dress. And her gold locket.
Her mother tied a big pink bow in her hair.
She was definitely prepared.

At ten minutes to seven Rudy drove them,

clean and shining, to Alyce's house. Then he went on to work.

"I hope it's something fun," said Rags, jumping up and down. "Like a party. Or a circus."

He and Angel were both remembering the wedding shower that Alyce had given for their mother. It was a costume party and Alyce was dressed like a Christmas tree.

But when Alyce answered the door, she was not dressed up. In fact, she looked surprised to see them. She had on old jeans and she had a dust mop in her hand.

"Why, come in!" she said. She looked like she wasn't sure she wanted company.

"Isn't it Friday?" asked Mrs. Pappadopolis.

"Is it?" said Alyce.

"Where's the sur——" Rags began to say. But as he spoke, his mother gently slipped her hand over his mouth.

"We've come to see your new couch," said Angel.

Now Alyce would have to admit the truth. When there was no couch she would have to call people out of hiding to shout surprise!

But to Angel's surprise, she said instead, "Here it is." And there in the living room where her old brown couch had stood was a brand new blue floral couch!

"What do you think?" said Alyce. "Do you like it?"

"It's lovely," their mother was saying. "Just lovely."

This was a surprise! It was not the surprise they expected. But a real new couch, as Alyce had said, was indeed a surprise. The surprise was on them.

Rags was starting to climb up on the couch and sit down. His mother grabbed him by his new T-shirt.

"Keep off of it, Rags. It's brand new."

The three guests stood around the couch and admired it. Then there seemed to be nothing to do but go home. And they would have to walk! Rudy had taken the car to work!

Angel was wondering why Alyce did not say, "Would you like a cup of coffee?" to her mother. Alyce always offered coffee. And soda pop for children. And a treat. Alyce always had a treat of some kind. But today she did not offer a thing.

"Well, I guess we'll start for home," said her mother.

"But we're all dressed up," whined Rags. "We can't go home."

"Keep quiet, Rags," whispered Angel. Even though Rags was right. They were all dressed up with no place to go.

"Well, we'll get going then," repeated Angel's mother. This time she started for the door. Alyce opened the door for them to leave — she seemed anxious for their departure!

Angel knew that any moment someone would jump out and yell SURPRISE! Any minute. They'd better hurry. Rags was already out the door. Her mother hung around the door, like she too expected something else. But it did not happen. No one brought out a giant cake. No one popped out of a closet. No fancy baby presents wrapped in pink and blue were in sight.

"Well, good-bye then," said their mother.

"Thanks for coming," said Alyce. "See you soon." The door actually shut. The three guests in their good clothes started down the sidewalk and headed for home.

"Mom, you said —" began Rags. Their mother interrupted.

"Well, I was wrong," said their mother. "That's what I get for expecting things. A person should not expect things. It was just that Alyce is always such a joker. She usually is playing some kind of trick. But I was wrong this time. She did want us to see her new couch."

They walked home in silence, Rags skipping and climbing on low walls and scaling them.

"Well, we had a fine walk and some good

exercise," said their mother when they finally came to their own house.

It was funny Alyce did not offer to drive them home, thought Angel. She had a car. It was not like her to let them walk.

"We'll just take these clothes off and get into our jeans and put some hamburgers on the grill," said Mrs. Pappadopolis in a false happy voice. She took the key out of her purse to open the door. But it wasn't locked. "Dear me, we forgot to lock the door when we left," she said.

Angel was surprised. Her mother was not forgetful. When the door opened, a shower of colored confetti fell on their heads. A giant baby picture of Angel, and one of Rags, hung on the wall! And what sounded like a hundred voices shouted, "SURPRISE!"

"I don't believe it!" said their mother.

There in the dining room near a table of delicious food stood Alyce, still in her jeans! And

Edna! And Rudy! And Margaret Toomer, and a roomful of other friends and neighbors! Baby presents were piled high on the sofa, and colored balloons hung everywhere.

"Are you surprised? Are you surprised?" shouted Alyce.

"I'm not," said Rags. "I knew there was a party. Otherwise, why would I be wearing this?" He pointed to his new outfit.

Everyone roared with laughter.

But Angel's mother said, "Yes, we are *very* surprised! We couldn't be more surprised."

"Having you come to my house was a red herring," said Alyce.

"What's a red herring?" asked Rags. "I didn't see any red herring."

"A red herring is a trick," said Rudy. "To mislead someone."

"To put them on the wrong track," said Alyce.

"Well, you certainly did that," their mother

said, laughing. "How in the world did you do all this?"

"Very quickly," Rudy said cheerfully. "I turned right around and got to work hanging decorations. And everyone brought this good food."

"We thought it would just be a party for the baby," said Alyce. "Not a traditional shower. Because we had a shower last year."

Everyone sat down and Rudy began to pass the dishes of good food around. There were hot dishes and potato salad and ham and cake and cookies. There were little sandwiches in the shape of rattles, and napkins folded like diapers. The paper plates and tablecloth had pictures of babies and baby toys all over them.

After dinner they played bingo, and Rudy called the numbers. After that they sang around the piano. And last of all, their mother opened the beautiful presents!

"Alyce has good parties," said Rags, his

face covered with chocolate ice cream, his hands sticky from gumdrops.

"For she's a jolly good fellow," sang Rudy, and all the others joined in.

"As nobody can deny!"

9.
Angel Takes a Spill

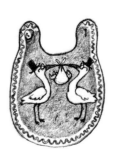

After all the guests had gone home, Angel and Rags helped Rudy clean the living room. Mrs. Pappadopolis arranged baby toys in cupboards and made neat piles of tiny sunsuits and bonnets.

"We have a lot of sleepers," she said, holding up a pale pink suit that to Angel looked like a washcloth with snaps and feet in it. "We'll have to get some baby bibs."

"We have one!" came a muffled voice.

Rags's head popped out of a box of crumpled tissue paper and ribbons. Curled ribbons hung from his ears. "Here's a bib," he said. "Edna brought it."

Rags was trying to smooth the plastic bib into a fold, but it only crackled and bounced back into its own shape again.

"That's one," said their mother. "We will need lots of bibs.

"I wonder where those little bibs of yours are," she said, frowning. "There was one darling bib with little storks in corners that Grandma made for you, Angel."

Her voice trailed off as she got up and headed upstairs.

Just yesterday after dinner, Rudy had warned Angel and Rags that soon the baby would be coming. He told them they all would have to watch their mother carefully. No steep stairs, no running to answer the door, no lifting.

So Angel followed her mother. She didn't want her to be alone in some part of the house where something could happen. Where she could trip or fall or get bumped. The baby could decide to come at home. That would surely be the last thing Angel wanted to worry about. The hospital was the place a baby came. With doctors around and nurses. No, Angel did not want to be the one in charge. Rudy said babies came when they were least expected. When you were off guard. And Angel knew this from watching "Family Ties" on TV. She had to watch her mother every minute these days. If Rudy and Rags were too busy picking up streamers and vacuuming up confetti, then it was up to Angel to watch.

She followed her mother to the bedroom. By the time she got there, her mother was already standing on a chair in her closet. She was reaching over her head for a box on the shelf. Angel rushed into the closet and called up to her.

"I'll do that. Let me get the box down."

Angel's mother bent down to lean on Angel's shoulder. She eased herself down from the chair. Her hair was tousled and her face was flushed.

Angel led her to the bed and smoothed a place on the edge for her to sit down.

"Rudy says no steps or ladders or chairs!" said Angel.

Her mother smiled. "I was looking for that little bib, Angel. The one with the storks that you and Rags used to wear. Grandma embroidered it by hand when you were born."

"I'll look," said Angel.

Angel climbed on the chair and stood on tiptoe. She could reach only the bottom shelf. Darn. She wanted to be a help to her mother. Why wasn't she taller? She stretched and reached, but it was still out of grasp.

All she could reach was an old yellow teddy bear and some rattles. The new baby had plenty of rattles.

Then she had an idea. She would take a hanger and poke the box. If she could slide it over, she could reach it. She poked and prodded and sure enough! It worked. The box slid forward.

Closer, closer — she almost had it! Just when her fingers were an inch away, there was a CRASH! Down on top of Angel came not only the box of baby clothes, but plastic shoe

boxes and heavy things. Bang, crash, plop. All on top of Angel.

Angel felt herself falling forward into a row of her mother's dresses. She tried to grab the shelf, but her fingers slipped and she fell to the floor with a crash on top of the shoe racks.

"Angel!" shouted her mother. "Oh, dear, why did I let you do that?"

Angel lay on the floor of the closet smelling her mother's cologne on the dresses. Voices sounded far away to her. In another land.

"Rudy, Rudy, come quick!" Angel heard her mother shouting.

"I'm all right," Angel tried to call. She must be all right because she could smell Evening in Paris. She could smell leather and mothballs too. And she felt cold wire hangers pressing against her arms. Her head hurt just a little bit. She must have bumped it on the way down. One of her arms ached, but if she could rub it, it would be OK.

She felt herself being lifted from the tangle

of clothes. She tried to open her eyes and say she was fine, but she couldn't seem to open either her eyes or her mouth. She heard doors being opened and closed. Opened and closed. Someone's hand was on her forehead. Maybe if she just slept for a little while. Just a little while. When she woke up she'd be able to find that bib with the storks.

When Angel opened her eyes, the first thing she saw was Rags's smiling face very close to her own. Too close.

"She's awake! She's awake!" he shrieked, and began bouncing against Angel's bed.

It did not look like Angel's bed! The sheets were crisp and white and did not have rows of pink rosebuds. Behind Rags was a blue curtain hanging from metal rings. She saw four legs under the curtain. Maybe they were at a school play. Maybe they were in the first row, where you could see the feet of the actors up close. She and Edna often saw the actors' feet and legs even when the curtains were closed.

But these legs did not belong to actors. They wore white stockings and white-laced shoes. Angel smelled medicine.

These were nurse's legs! Angel was in a hospital room!

Rudy came up and kissed both her cheeks.

"You took an awful spill!" he said. "Do you remember?"

Angel remembered rows of shoes. And the smell of the clothes.

"I didn't find the bib," she said.

"You fell off the chair," said Rudy, "and had a slight concussion, and you broke your arm. The doctor set it, and you've been in the hospital overnight."

A concussion sounded serious. And a broken arm! How could she have done this? Not only didn't she find the bib for her mother, but she broke bones and had to come to the hospital! Instead of helping her mother, she had made new problems. Angel sighed.

When she looked down at her arm, she saw

a hard white cast up to her elbow! How could she hold the baby now? How could she be of help when the baby came? She hoped it was off her arm before the baby arrived.

And where was her mother? Why wasn't she here? Angel knew. Her mother was cross with her for not finding the bib. And for making so much trouble. A tear rolled down her face.

Rags crawled out from under the bed where he had been pretending to be a lizard. He slid across the slippery, waxed floor and then came to inspect Angel's cast. He gave it a few good knocks and then turned his attention to the water jug on the bedside table.

"It will heal fast," said Rudy. "The doctor said it was a simple fracture."

Simple was not the word Angel would have chosen. If it was simple she would not be here in the hospital. And her mother would not be cross with her.

The blue curtain swished and a nurse came

in. She had curly red hair and round pink cheeks.

"My name's Rita. How are we this morning?" she said, smiling at Angel.

Did she mean all of them? Rudy, Rags, Angel, and Rita? Or just Rita and Angel?

"Everyone's all right but me," said Angel. "I have a broken arm."

Rita laughed.

Rags raised and lowered the lid on the water jug.

Rita shook a thermometer and placed it under Angel's tongue. It felt cold.

"Does your arm still hurt?" asked Rita.

Angel nodded. The thermometer wiggled up and down.

Rita put two small orange pills in a fluted cup and handed them to Angel. Then she poured a glass of water and took the thermometer out of Angel's mouth.

"Just chew these and you'll start to feel better," she said.

Angel took the pills and then lay back on her pillow. She wondered if Edna had ever been in the hospital. If she had ever broken any bones or had a slight concussion. Angel was pretty sure she had.

"We'll be seeing your mom in a minute," said Rudy.

What? Was her mom here after all? And if she was, why was she hiding?

Rudy stepped out into the hall for a moment and then he called in to Angel, "I'll be back in no time flat." He waved.

Rags was busy identifying items in the bed-side cupboard. He showed Angel packets of moist towelettes, a stack of paper cups, plastic straws that bent where they had little accordion pleats.

"I could use these for my city," he said. "For street lights. And buildings," he went on.

"You can't take those, Rags. They belong to the hospital."

Angel found it hard to get interested in cups

and straws. How could Rags be so cheerful when his sister was in a cast in the hospital? Didn't Rags worry about what had happened to their mother while they were not there to watch over her? Suddenly Angel felt very lonesome for her mother. She wanted her to burst through the door right now and tell her how much she loved her. And that she forgave her for all the trouble she made.

Rags was pestering her about taking some straws home.

"Rags, you can't take things that don't belong to you." But the more Angel thought about it, the more she thought maybe it was like going to a restaurant and taking home sugar packets with pictures of wildlife on them, even though you ordered milk and didn't need to use them. Maybe it was expected, that people would take these things, as souvenirs! That's what Edna had once said when she was at the beach with Angel and Rags carrying a towel with IRONHEAD INN on it.

She had told them that when you go on vacation it was OK to take small things from motels you stayed at, like little soaps, shampoos, and bathcaps. Angel wondered at the time if a towel was a "little" thing, but she didn't want to pursue it. Edna would think Angel had never vacationed or stayed at motels.

Rags was now trying to balance a steel bedpan on top of his head.

Just then Rudy appeared, pushing a shiny wheelchair.

"Get in!" he said, pointing to the chair. "You are going for a little ride!"

10.
Baby Talk

The wheelchair was for Angel! She felt excited thinking of riding in it, but worried about where in the world they were going. It couldn't be far. You couldn't go out of the hospital and down the street, surely, in a wheelchair. Or to get hamburgers at a drive-in.

Rudy looked very cheerful for someone who had a daughter with a broken arm.

She got into the wheelchair as Rudy directed. Rags began to pout and his lower lip began to tremble as it did before he began to cry.

"Can Rags ride too?" asked Rudy, looking at Rags's sad face.

Angel sighed. She couldn't even enjoy a broken arm, or a hospital stay alone, she thought. Even this she had to share with her brother. But she moved over in the wheelchair and made room for him. "Watch out for my cast," was all she said.

"Here we go," said Rudy, gripping the handles of the wheelchair.

"Off we go! Off we go!" called Rags.

Maybe they were going to the hospital café for some pie, thought Angel. Or maybe they were taking a taxi to meet their mother. But Angel wasn't dressed.

"Faster, faster!" shouted Rags. Down the hall they went, the rubber wheels sailing along the smooth floor. Past the nurses' station, where Rita looked up and waved, past steel carts loaded with dinner trays.

"Beep, beep," shouted Rags whenever they came to someone ahead of them. Soon they came to an elevator, and Rudy pressed a button. Rags called out the lighted numbers over the door. "One, nine, four, three," he said.

Finally the doors opened and Rudy wheeled Angel and Rags onto the elevator. Two doctors were talking quietly and looking at a notebook.

"Press fourth floor, Angel," said Rudy. Angel pressed the four with her good arm. What could be on four?

When the door opened on four, they rolled into a hall that looked like the floor Angel was on, except for the walls. These walls were decorated with little animals carrying the letters of the alphabet. Blue and pink and yellow and green. Dogs and cats and giraffes and elephants.

Before they knew it, they were in a room where the walls were all pink. They stopped by a bed, and in the bed was their mother!

"Angel!" cried Mrs. Pappadopolis. She reached out her arms to give Angel a big hug.

She wasn't cross with Angel after all! She

was glad to see her! Why was she here then, instead of in Angel's room with the rest of them?

Angel saw that she was wearing her good yellow robe that Rudy had given her for Christmas. Her hair was different from usual. It was brushed back from her face and tied with a yellow ribbon. She surely did not look sick. If anything, she looked healthier than ever. There was no medicine by her bed, and no casts or bandages in sight.

Suddenly Angel knew why her mother was in the hospital. Why hadn't she thought of it sooner!

"Right after you broke your arm," said Rudy, "the baby decided to come. All three of you landed in the hospital at once."

Rudy walked around to the other side of the bed and uncovered a tiny blanket beside her mother. Angel hadn't even noticed it was there, it was so small.

"Meet your new sister!" said Rudy.

A sister! Even though Angel had been waiting for the baby, she couldn't believe she had one! And so fast. One day they were all playing games and eating potato salad, and the next day here was the baby! It must be very easy to get a baby. And they must arrive very, very fast.

Angel and Rags got out of the wheelchair and walked over to the bed.

When they saw their sister, their real, live, new baby, even Rags was speechless.

Rudy picked up the baby carefully and placed her in Angel's good arm. Rudy held the baby's head. Angel remembered from the classes how weak a baby's head was.

Angel looked down at this baby that came so suddenly into their life. No matter how many toys and bibs and sleepers — no matter how many rooms were made ready for her — this baby was still a surprise.

She was a real person now, with real eyes

and nose and mouth and little fingers, and feelings. Just like Angel.

Angel couldn't tell that she was girl — no

long curly hair or long eyelashes. In fact, she was so red she looked like a plum. Not like anyone in the family.

"How do we know it's a girl?" said Rags finally.

Rags was right. What if, in addition to not being a girl, it wasn't even their baby? Could the doctor have made a mistake?

"The doctors were very careful," Rudy said. "Here's the plastic bracelet that every baby wears." Angel and Rags looked at the little bracelet, which read, "Baby Girl Pappadopolis."

"We have to think of a name for your sister," said their mother.

"This is a family decision," said Rudy. "She belongs to all of us."

Angel couldn't think of any names good enough for their own baby. At least the baby wouldn't be Burt. Rags's eyebrows came together in a frown. He was probably trying to think up a Burt-like name for a girl, thought

Angel. And Allan would be out, much to Alyce's dismay.

A name should have meaning. After all, it would be the baby's name forever, even when she grew up and got married. She couldn't even smile yet. What if this baby grew up and did not like her name? What if she discovered that it was Angel who had named her? Angel wanted the baby to like her. She decided to leave it up to her mother and father and Rags.

"How about Bertie?" he said hopefully.

By the time the nurse poked her head in the door to say that supper would be served in ten minutes (and that Rudy, Rags, and Angel could stay), they had decided on the name Athena.

No one but Rudy liked the name at first. Rags couldn't pronounce it even when Rudy wrote it for him in capital letters on a piece of paper. And Angel thought it sounded too much like furniture polish or floor wax. It was one of those names, she thought, that sounded foreign. When you heard it you could never say, "Oh, I know someone named that." Girls Angel knew had names like Sara or Sally or Lori. But Mrs. Pappadopolis and Rudy liked it. Angel wanted them to be happy. It was the least she could do to pretend to like it. It might even grow on her in time, she thought.

Angel looked down at Athena, cuddled on the bed. Her eyes were closed.

"Isn't she tiny and sweet," mused her mother. Angel waited for her mother to say, "She looks just like you did when you were born, Angel," but she didn't. Instead she said, "She is much darker than you and Rags were."

Angel was relieved to hear that. She hoped she had never looked like a plum. Even as a newborn baby.

Athena made a little gurgling noise.

"She likes her name," said her mother.

"Athena Pappadopolis," said Rudy with a

smile. "It was my grandmother's name. She lived in Greece."

Now Angel realized why it sounded so foreign! It was! Greece was far away. It was a place where a man tried to fly but got too close to the sun and his wax wings melted and he fell into the sea. Angel never liked that story. Poor little Athena. Would she be Greek too?

"Athena was also the name of a goddess," said Rudy.

"What's a goddess?" asked Rags. "What's a thena?"

"Not a thena," said Rudy. "It's all one word."

Rags frowned. Bertie would be easier.

"Couldn't we call her Thena for short?" asked Angel.

"What a good idea!" said her mother. "You'd like that, wouldn't you, Thena?" she said to the sleeping bundle. Her voice sounded like baby talk. Like when Rags was little. Angel hoped her mother would outgrow this way of talking.

"Thena it is!" cried Rudy.

Mrs. Pappadopolis's supper was brought in, along with Angel's and also food for the guests. Angel's tray had her room number on it. Rudy held Athena while their mother ate supper.

After supper Rags fell asleep on the bottom of the bed. Athena did too. Angel and her mother talked about the accident and how glad everyone was that she was all right. "I couldn't believe it when we ended up in the hospital together!" she said.

"All's well that ends well," said Rudy, laughing.

"That sounds like something Alyce would say," Angel agreed, laughing too.

"I can still help with the baby with my cast on," said Angel, hoping her mother wouldn't think she had to take care of three children as soon as she got home.

"You just rest up, you and your mom," said Rudy. "We are going to have someone come in and help out for the first few weeks till we get organized. Maybe Alyce."

Oh no! thought Angel. If Alyce came to help out, they would *never* get organized. Last time she had helped out, *she* ended up in this very hospital!

"We have to sign your cast," said their mother. "Athena and I will be the first."

Rudy got a pen out of his pocket. After her mother signed her name and Thena's name, Rudy signed too. He drew a little picture of Angel in a wheelchair.

"I wanna write too," said Rags sleepily.

Rudy held Rags's hand while he wrote RAGS in big black letters.

Just then a nurse popped through the door.

"You have visitors," she announced. The door opened wider and in walked Alyce, Edna, and Margaret Toomer! Edna was almost hidden behind a big bouquet of flowers!

"Hello, hello!" called Alyce. She had a large pink carnation pinned to her blouse. "We've just been to the nursery to see him. He is adorable!"

"He's beautiful!" added Margaret Toomer.

At that moment, Athena began to cry.

Alyce's eyes grew wide. "What's this? Another baby? Twins!"

Angel's mother laughed. "No, this is the only one. Angel and Rags have a new little sister!"

"She's a thena," said Rags.

"Then what about Allan? Rudy told us the baby's name began with A."

"I think you were looking at the wrong baby, Alyce. Rudy, show them Athena."

"Athena? What kind of name is that?" said Edna.

"It's Greek," said Angel. "It's the name of a goddess."

Edna seemed impressed, thought Angel. At least she didn't know another baby with that name! She looked impressed with Angel's cast too. "My cousin had one," she said. "He fell out of an apple tree." But she looked envious of Angel's wheelchair.

"And I have to keep this cast on for a long time," said Angel.

"Coochi coochi coo!" Alyce was saying to the baby. She and Margaret took turns holding Athena in their arms. Edna jumped up from admiring Angel's cast to have her turn holding the baby.

"So you and your mother ended up here together!" said Alyce.

Angel nodded.

"It never rains but it pours!" said Alyce wisely.

Alyce had a saying for every occasion, it seemed to Angel.

Then a nurse looked in and said visiting hours were over and she had to take Athena back to the nursery. The visitors said goodbye. It seemed very quiet after they'd gone.

Angel was anxious to get home and have the entire family back where they belonged. She was impatient to pack her things in the plastic bag that said "Patient's Belongings."

She had a lot of arranging to do if she was going to fit all her "souvenirs" in with her bathrobe and slippers and flowers.

And she had a lot of thinking to do. About her sudden new family. She would always be the oldest one in the family, and that was a lot of responsibility. Why, even Rags was not yet as old as her subscription to *Child's Day* magazine. And it would take time to adjust to the fact she could put "one" on the blanks at school that said "sisters." And size of family: "five." For so long she had put "three" there, then "four," and now it changed again. Soon the table would be set for five instead of four. And instead of the three of them waiting for just Rags to hop in the car, they would be waiting for someone even younger.

Rita came to wheel Angel back to her room,

so she stopped thinking and kissed her mother good night. When they passed the nursery Angel looked in at Athena sleeping peacefully in her little glass bed.

Angel felt a warm, happy feeling watching the baby sleep. She wondered how she could have ever thought of running away from home just because a baby was coming. Things can't always stay the same. Families change. Three children was the perfect size for a family.

Especially since two of them were girls!

11.
Just a Dream

The next day it was time for the Pappadopolis family to go home. Rita came to wheel Angel to the front door. But first she gave her a red sling with silver buckles on it.

"Now that you will be moving around a lot, you'll need to be careful about your cast. This will help hold it in place."

Then they were off. Angel climbed into the wheelchair. Her last ride down the shiny hall. In her lap, instead of Rags, she held her plastic bag of clothes and the bouquet Edna had brought her.

They got on the elevator, and Angel pushed G for ground floor. That was the main entrance where they were to meet her mother and Thena. Sure enough, when the doors opened, there they were! Her mother sat in a wheelchair too. In her arms was Thena. Her eyes were wide open and she was making gurgling noises! Thena did not look so red today. And not so wrinkled. She looked like a real baby instead of a plum.

Angel and her mother sat side by side in their wheelchairs. It felt good to be outside in the sunshine. More nurses came out to say good-bye. It looked like the whole nurses' station from Angel's floor were here! They all crowded around to look at Thena and admire Angel's new red sling.

"I wonder where Rudy is," said Angel's mother. "He was supposed to be here by now."

Angel hoped he would come soon. She didn't want her mother to worry. She closed her eyes and told herself that when she opened them, Rudy's car would be turning into the

driveway. If it wasn't, then Angel herself
would have to start to worry.

Maybe the car had engine trouble. It wasn't
long ago that Angel had pictured Rudy's clown
car splitting in half —

Just then a car horn sounded. Angel opened
her eyes and saw the car coming toward them.
Balloons were flying from the windows, red
and yellow and blue ones. Probably balloons
from Alyce's party, thought Angel. Rags was

leaning out the front window, waving more balloons.

The car stopped and Rudy jumped out. Around his neck was a camera.

"Hold it!" he shouted. "We have to get a picture of this. It won't ever happen again."

Angel smiled, and wondered what wouldn't happen again. The baby? A broken arm? How could Rudy be so sure?

Click! went Rudy's camera.

Then they were all in the car waving. They were on the way home. Angel felt as if she'd been away for months. Had it really been only three days? Rags was jumping up and down in the front seat. He kept turning to Thena and saying, "There's my kindergarten" or "There's the library," as Rudy drove down Main Street. Angel wondered if she'd see anyone she knew. She was anxious to show her friends her new baby sister.

At last the car pulled up into their own driveway. Angel and Rags jumped out. Rudy lifted Athena into his arms and took their mother by the hand up the steps to the front door. When they got inside, Angel expected to see the house just as she left it. With crumpled wrapping paper and streamers and deflated balloons on the living room floor. And her mother's room in a mess. But it wasn't. The only thing left from the party were the giant pictures of Angel and Rags. Someone (probably Alyce) had added the words, "Welcome home, Athena!" The words came out of Angel's and Rags's mouth, like in the comic strips. The whole house had been cleaned, and in the middle of the dining room table was a huge white cake with pink icing. Beside it was a tiny baby dress. And the booties Angel had made. Next to that was a dainty bib all starched and white with the two storks on it! Hanging in the doorway between the dining room and kitchen was the baby swing. It seemed ages ago when Edna and Rags and Angel had helped Alyce carry it in from her car.

"I want a piece of cake," said Rags. Angel hoped he would not start to whine already on their first night home.

"We'll all have cake, Rags," said their mother. "But first Thena has to eat. When she gets a little bigger, you will be feeding her."

Thena was starting to cry. It was the first time Angel had seen her cry. Really cry. Her little mouth was open and her face turned bright red. Angel's mother put on an apron and went to the kitchen. Angel heard the sounds of bottles and pans and boiling water.

As soon as the nipple was in Thena's mouth she stopped crying and sucked the milk down noisily.

"She was starving!" said Angel.

That night, after everyone was in bed, even Athena, Angel heard a noise in the bathroom.

"Rags, what are you doing?" asked Angel, wondering why the first-aid kit was open on the edge of the bathtub. The roll of gauze was trailing across the sink and toilet.

"I'm making a cast," said Rags. "For my arm."

Sure enough, there was Rags with his dirty little arm up to its elbow in some kind of white paste. Angel noticed a white puddle around Rags's feet and saw an empty bottle of Elmer's glue lying on its side.

"See, glue and water make plaster," said Rags. "First you wrap the bandage, then you cover it with plaster. Now I have a cast like yours."

What a sight! And their mother just home from the hospital. She needed peace and quiet. If Rags wasn't whining about cake, he was busy making messes in plaster. Poor Rags. Angel and their mother and Thena had all the attention. Angel felt like she wanted to hug him, but as an older sister she had to set a good example. She surely didn't want her mother or Rudy to see this mess.

"Let's clean up the bathroom, Rags. I'll get you a cloth sling."

She was pretty sure that the paste wouldn't harden, and even if it did get crusty, Rags wouldn't be able to take a bath or run under the sprinkler for weeks. The thought of Rags walking around town with his arm in a dirty homemade cast wasn't very appealing to Angel. A clean sling from an old sheet would be much more suitable. Angel sighed. A sister's job was never done.

Later, after Rags had been showered, scrubbed, and put to bed freshly bandaged, Angel lay in her own bed. She thought of the days to come. Of Thena in little sunsuits. Thena in Rags's dirt city. Thena toddling behind Angel. Angel would teach her to walk. To say her name. To ride a bike. Rags would be in real school. She tried to picture Rags in school. But in her mind he was still short. Still whining. Would he ever grow up?

Angel was sleepy. It was nice to be back in her bed with the rosebud sheets. Rags was asleep. Thena was safely tucked into her crib downstairs. Her parents were in the room below hers watching TV. In the distance she thought she could hear a phone ringing. Must be next door, or on TV. Or in a dream.

Sounds of her parents' voices, speaking low, drifted upstairs. Half asleep, Angel heard snatches of conversation.

Words like "christening" and "Greece" floated in the night air. For a while there was no sound. Then her mother's voice seemed to say, "We won't tell Angel yet."

It was just a dream, of course.

Angel turned over and fell asleep.